T0209596

To Swim Like a Fish

GWEN KING

AuthorHouse™
1663 Liberty Drive
Bloomington, IN 47403
www.authorhouse.com
Phone: 1 (800) 839-8640

Published by AuthorHouse 07/12/2019

ISBN: 978-1-7283-1854-7 (sc)
ISBN: 978-1-7283-1853-0 (e)

Library of Congress Control Number: 2019909251

Print information available on the last page.

Any people depicted in stock imagery provided by Getty Images are models,
and such images are being used for illustrative purposes only.
Certain stock imagery © Getty Images.

This book is printed on acid-free paper.

Because of the dynamic nature of the Internet, any web addresses or links contained in this book may have changed
since publication and may no longer be valid. The views expressed in this work are solely those of the author and do
not necessarily reflect the views of the publisher, and the publisher hereby disclaims any responsibility for them.

authorHOUSE®

Author's Acknowledgement

Gwen wishes to give special thanks to her son, Deen who gave her encouragement to seize the moment "to start writing now and not later". To her brother, Everton, who critique her stories and evoked memories of their childhood. To her specials friends (Sista) M Astonia Brown and Hermia Morton- Anthony who provided positive feedback when needed; and to Ian M Queely who offered laughter and inspiration to make the story happen.

Montclair was not taking no for an answer. He wanted to swim in the sea. He was very excited. Today was the day he would go to the beach with his mom, but she would not allow him to go alone in the water. As they walked from the house, she held on to his hand real tight. He could not get out of her grasp.

The beach was his most favorite place in the world. He loved to feel the waves splashing on his feet. He liked to see the many fishes swimming next to him. They even brushed his legs as they swam by. The water was so clear he could see right down to the bottom. He had tried many times to catch a fish, but they always slipped through his fingers. He wanted to swim like a fish but had to figure out how. Now, that was a puzzle!

When he was swimming in the sea, his mom always told him to keep his head above water. She did not want him to drown. He wondered why he had to keep his head above water; the fish that swam by him had their heads underwater, but they did not drown. Montclair thought that if he could swim like a fish, then his mom would not keep reminding him to keep his head above water.

Thinking very hard about the puzzle, he told himself that maybe if he studied the fish, he might be able to discover their secret. He watched and watched as the fish swam. He noticed that they wiggled their tails and fluttered those things on their sides that looked like wings. He remembered that his dad said they were called fins. Now he had to figure out how the fish kept their heads underwater and did not drown. He had to figure it out.

Montclair was playing in the yard with his puppy when he heard his mom call. "Montclair, Montclair", she called, "get ready! We are leaving for the beach."

They began walking along the street with cars parked on both sides of the road, when his Mom met Mrs. Smithy. Mrs. Smithy lived up the road from them. She was heading to town dressed in a bright-red dress and with her head wrapped with a multicolored head tie. She was on her way to the bus stop, but Montclair thought she had forgotten to put on her closed-up dress shoes because she was wearing sandals with all her toes out.

Mrs. Smithy had just come back from Canada, where she had been visiting her grandchildren. Lord, she could chat! She shared all the news from the time she got on the plane, what happened when she got to Canada, and all the things she did when she got up there. She mentioned the names of the grandchildren, whom they looked like, and how they liked West Indian food, which she cooked every day.

She talked about the salt fish and johnnycake, the pig tail and red peas soup, and how she had to go the West Indian store to find pig tail. Now, to Montclair that didn't make any sense; he wondered why Mrs. Smithy couldn't just go to a store like the one in town and find her pig tail.

Mrs. Smithy suddenly said, her face lighting up with a smile, as she giggled, "girl, everybody loved my fried plantains. I fried them just so."

Montclair tried to get his mom's attention. He pulled her hand to keep walking, but she pulled him back without missing a beat in the conversation. The conversation might go on all day because his mom began to talk about what happened when she went to the States, how cold it was even though it was early summer, how she drove with her older son for twelve hours from Baltimore to Atlanta, how long the ride was, how she fell asleep in the car, and how hot Atlanta was at that time of the year. Lord, what a thing! Montclair thought at the rate they were going, he would not be able to go into the sea.

A car passed by and the group moved and stepped under a mango tree.

Montclair looked at the tree laden with mangoes and saw a lizard, a bright green lizard lying on the trunk of the mango tree. It had brown specks on its back. Its tail was curled up. It was lying quietly and appeared to be staring at him. Then all of a sudden the lizard puffed its throat out. Montclair jumped with surprise. His eyes opened with wonder. That was amazing! He had never seen a lizard do that before. The lizard continued to stare at him and then Montclair heard a soft rustle in the grass on the ground below the tree. Another green lizard leaped from the grass onto the trunk of the tree and began crawling to the lizard with the puffed out throat.

Montclair turned back to his mom and pulled her hand again to get her attention. But she pulled him back to her like an elastic band. While still listening to Mrs. Smithy, she said, "Boy, keep still! Don't you see me talking? Learn some manners!"

Montclair's mom then asked Mrs. Smithy, "Do you know how to make fish soup without bones?"

Mrs. Smithy said, "Sure, I know how to make fish soup." But when Montclair's mother asked for the recipe, Mrs. Smithy said, "Lord, child you know me; I don't cook with a recipe. It is a little of this and a little of that, and the food turns out all right."

They decided that one day, Mrs. Smithy would come by and show his mom how to cook fish soup.

Montclair tried again to get his mother's attention and pulled at the bottom of her pink blouse. She smacked him on his hands and said, "What's your problem? Don't you see me speaking? Learn some manners! Don't let me tell you again!"

He wanted to go to the sea. He looked at her pink blouse and noticed that the blouse was torn where he had pulled it. He hoped his mother would not notice, and he tried to tuck it into the capri by pretending that he was playing. Then he turned to his mom and said, "I am sorry, Mom. The reason I pulled you is because I would like to go to the beach."

As he spoke, he noticed that the lizards were now chasing one another along the mango tree branches. He smiled because they seem to be having so much fun playing hide and seek.

At last his mom turned to Mrs. Smithy and said, "See you later, and don't forget to come by to show me how to cook the fish soup."

Mrs. Smithy said, "Yes, yes, I'm going to come, and I will call you before and tell you what to buy."

Montclair was happy. His mom and him continued their walk to the beach. They passed the golden apple tree by the small river in the village and then the Methodist church, and made a right by Mr. Johnson's shop. His mother said good morning to everyone on the road, and he was praying that she did not stop to chat again.

When they reached the beach, Montclair rushed to get out of his clothes and go into the water. He was wearing his short khaki pants with a merino shirt, but he had worn his black trunks under his clothes. He rushed into the sea; his mom was right behind him in her red bathing suit, the one his aunt sent last Christmas in a box from the States.

Montclair plunged into the waves and then came back up. He decided to swim like a fish. He put his head under the water, and the water went up his nose and down his mouth. He came back up sputtering. He decided that he would keep his mouth shut, keep his feet together, and move them up and down like a fish. But he began to sink and could not swim. He could not figure out how to keep the water out of his nose. So he ducked under the water holding his nose, but with his mouth shut, he could not breathe.

Then he decided to hold his breath and flap his hands like the fins of the fish. He used a stone to mark his starting point to see how far he could swim. He held his breath, flapped his hands, and moved his feet up and down. He did not get very far.

When he came back up, his mom asked, "Boy, what are you doing? Stop skylarking; you could drown."

Montclair said, "I want to swim under water like the fish."
Then his mom said, "But you do not have gills to breathe through."

"Gills?" Montclair asked. "What are gills?"

His mom said, "Gills are like lungs to the fish. The gills take oxygen out of the water and carry away the carbon dioxide. Like humans, the fish need oxygen to breathe so that they can live underwater for a long time. But they cannot live out of water for a long time, because the oxygen they need to live can only be found in water. The gills will collapse, and the fish will not be able to breathe and will die.

"You, on the other hand, cannot stay underwater for a long time because you do not have gills. Humans have lungs, instead of gills, to breathe in oxygen from the air and to breathe out carbon dioxide. If they stay underwater for too long, water will get into their lungs, and they will drown and die."

Montclair was amazed to learn about how fish breathe through gills to swim. His mom explained that he could swim, but not like a fish; he had to keep his head above water. Then she said, "There is a way to swim underwater. It is called snorkeling. A mask goes over your eyes and nose. It is like wearing glasses with your nose covered up. You put a tube in your mouth that goes up above the water, so you can breathe through your mouth. You can only swim just below the surface of the water, because if you go deeper, water will get in the tube.

"If you want to swim in deeper water it is called scuba diving. For that, you will need a wetsuit to keep you dry and warm. It covers you from head to toe. You wear a mask similar to a snorkeling mask but different. A tube is also attached to your mouth, but it runs to a tank filled with oxygen, which is attached to your back. You can go deeper below the water and breathe in oxygen from the tank. This setup allows humans to continue to breathe and to stay underwater as long as the oxygen is available. Most of the time, scuba divers do not dive alone but with a master diver and others."

Montclair's mom promised him that she would teach him how to swim, and then he could learn how to swim under the water by holding his breath for a very short time. Then she said "when you are older, you can learn how to scuba dive and snorkel and swim with the fish."

Printed in the United States
By Bookmasters